I0764633

Praise for *Hunger and Other Stories*

"Wilson pulls at our emotions and hidden desires with a wide variety of characters."

—Annie Sargent, *The St. Augustine Record*

"The writer has a way with words...Each picture is dark with nothingness. The language and sexual scenes makes this adult reading."

—Reba Neighbors Collins, *The Sunday Oklahoman*

"The series of stories has some shining moments of forceful deeply felt description."

—Javier Bernal, *Semana Newspaper*

"These stories are unsettling because of their stark honesty. The frailty of human relationships and the vulnerability of grown-ups spanning a lifetime are a compelling subject."

—Uneza Akhter, *DAWN*

"This amazing use of language, and clarity of description, compels the reader on."

—Patricia Gulian, *Book/Mark*

"The poignant, well-written tales are loaded with depth rarely seen in short stories, turning the reader introspective pondering each story long after finishing them."

—Harriet Klausner, *The Midwest Book Review*

Great Things Are Coming

ALSO BY IAN RANDALL WILSON

Hunger and Other Stories
Out of the Arcadian Ghetto (fiction chapbook)
Theme of the Parabola (poetry chapbook)

Great Things Are Coming

a novella

Ian Randall Wilson

Hollyridge Press
Venice, California

 Published in the United States by Hollyridge Press.

Hollyridge Press
P.O. Box 2872
Venice, California 90294

Cover and Book Design and Author Photo by Rio Smyth
Manufactured in the United States of America by Lightning Source

Publisher's Cataloging-in-Publication
(Prepared by The Donohue Group, Inc.)

Wilson, Ian Randall.
Great things are coming : a novella / Ian Randall Wilson.

p. ; cm.

ISBN-13: 978-0-9799588-4-7
ISBN-10: 0-9799588-4-9

1. Clerks--Diaries--Fiction. 2. Temporary employees--Fiction. 3. Man-woman relationships--Fiction. I. Title.

PS3573.I456955 G7 2008
813/.6 2008931361

14 13 12 11 10 09 08 10 9 8 7 6 5 4 3 2 1

for Denise

I witness and wait.

—Walt Whitman

Acknowledgment

Originally published in *The Gettysburg Review.*

Great Things Are Coming

There was no carpet showing. The gray rug was completely covered by stacks of documents, some of them rising four feet high to form a scale model of an ancient Incan city of paper. He had audited several architecture courses and recognized the form: the land of four quarters, the contoured, terraced miniatures laid out and erected as integrated flights in white xerographic paper ornamented with inked reliefs of geometric and zoomorphic figures. Tan and green file folders bulged with white bond stepping down to a wider base. Loose sheets stuck out at angles, their surfaces marked by weird hieroglyphics and a golden sun logo on all the pieces of letterhead. How would he cross the eight feet from door to desk without destroying this construction? How would he even find the desk, its top buried by more stacks of files?

At his interview, Ms. Finestein in personnel told him that he was filling in for Lynette who had been with the company for fifty-three years. Lynette had pneumonia or something, maybe the flu, and she smoked. "You know how it is for old people," Ms. Finestein said.

He didn't know how it was for old people because he had tried to avoid them all his life. His parents lived far away, and he had been spared the distress of watching grandparents decay: they died in the war. Still, the image of slack skin, mottled hands, hunching walks—he couldn't bear to think he was headed for such a finish. He needed the work, so he nodded in agreement, and said, "Too bad. I hope she gets better."

"She's coming back," Ms. Finestein said. "You can bet the light. She'll be back."

He managed to tread a thin line along the wall, flattening himself back, and spreading his arms. He leaned and took exaggerated steps, testing his next move before applying full weight, bending his knees, never crossing his feet. The floor remained solid, and only one building toppled as he made his way across the room.

"You're going to have to do something about that," a voice called from the hall.

He clung to the desk's edge for balance and looked up into a tan, weather-beaten face, button nose, thin lips, skin sagging, marked with brown, the body flabby. She wore a gray skirt cut just below the knees, nylon hose, sensible shoes.

"You the temp?" she asked in a voice rubbed raw and hoarse from wind and cigarettes, too much scotch.

He nodded.

"Lent is almost over and we keep the liquor there." She inclined her head toward one of the cabinets. "Mr. J likes his afternoon splash and when he says, 'Sally, it's time,' well, you're blocking the path."

He nodded again as if to take on this responsibility too. There was enough room for him to pull back the chair and slip into it. The cushion supported his lumbar region, the fabric cool against his lower back and legs though the platform was set far too close to the ground for a person of his height.

Sally stayed at the door.

He said, "Do you have any idea…Ms. Finestein said…Is there someone who…"

He rummaged around in the drawers, looked on the shelves, opened cabinets, inspected books, eyed the desk.

"You won't find any job manual in there."

He stopped looking and turned back to her, placing his hands in his lap. She gestured at the room. "Lynette kept it all up here." She tapped her forehead. "Years and years up here. Good luck."

"Sally," he said, before she walked away. "What time is lunch?"

He found Lynette's number in a worn notebook and dialed but no one answered. After that he was not sure of what to do or how to begin. The immensity of the work was paralyzing, so many files, so much paper. This had to be what made Lynette sick.

He looked at the telephone hoping someone would call with instructions—or a reprieve. He should have turned down the assignment. He should have asked for work in a different industry. He should have been more specific about his exact job needs instead of accepting the first thing that came along, one with an indefinite period that might go on "for weeks" the woman at the temporary agency said in a whisper. "This is a good one, at a good company. It could turn into something."

Everyone hoped that every assignment *turned into something*. When that happened, the temp got permanent employment, the agency got a substantial finder's fee for the placement and a percentage of the new employee's salary for the first year—satisfaction all around.

Lynette's office was small, filled with cocoa-colored wood furniture and plants drooping from lack of water. He counted six ashtrays, each appropriated from a different hotel. Outside the door, people walked by, glancing in at him. They were curious. They said nothing. They looked at the floor, at the piles of paper, back up to him. One or two smiled. Another one coughed. How should he interpret a cough? He wanted to close the door and escape those looks, but the gesture might be misread: the unsupervised temp taking advantage, loafing on company time, taking money and not doing any work. Instead, he continued to look around the office, opening a cabinet to find a trio of ceramic lions and a red Webster's dictionary.

In the top right drawer, a set of rosary beads lay curled among a stack of file cards and some slips of worn paper covered by an unreadable green scrawl. Below were religious medallions. On the shelf in front, a metal crucifix hung above a word processor, the machine's amber screen blank. Jesus bless the clerks.

He understood computers. He reached behind and turned it on. The disk drives hummed and the amber screen flickered to life, then the machine beeped and flashed greetings. He managed to logon and page through the directory.

"You won't find much there," Sally's voice called from the door again. "She hates that thing. Can't use it. Didn't you call her yet?"

Sally was correct; the computer's directory told him nothing of what Lynette might do. Lucky for him, it contained software that he was intimately familiar with, and an attempt at a meager tutorial. He called Lynette again. He let the phone ring twenty times.

He had to begin somewhere, so he started sorting the stacks. The loose documents he tried to order by project, by the heading printed somewhere at the top of all of them though they made no sense: "Feeler Replicator," "Doneagain Milestone Reunion," "Anchove Reclamation Works." Contracts, proposals, reports, memoranda, letters, audit summaries. He had asked for general office work, especially wordprocessing—anything was better than waiting tables. The agency told him that the company was some kind of foundation, giving money over a wide yet eclectic range of undertakings. It was private. It had been around for a long, long time. It had "old money."

There were many duplicates of each document, as if no one was convinced the right copy would reach the right place, ever, and sent another along just to be sure. The redundancy reached ten on some of the documents.

He located a datestamp that printed the date in red and Lynette's name in blue. He read the heading on each document, date-stamped, then separated them into more piles. Loose sheets went into folders. In three hours the desk was clear, the piles moved into other stacks organized by his own system into the space behind him. No one answered at Lynette's home.

Then it was time for lunch.

He was lost and there was no room 7102—no longer a room 7102 because, of course, there had been one earlier; he sat in it all morning. Now he couldn't find it. He ended up in accounting where a man wearing a gray suit said, "Not here." The golden sun logo spread across the breast pocket matching another woven into the fabric of the partitions surrounding the cubicle creating a regular motif. "I don't really know," the man said. "I haven't been here that long. Did you ask at reception?"

The next attempt brought him back to human resources. "How's everything going?" Ms. Finestein said. She came around from her desk and paused at her door, fingering the material of a gray blazer hanging on a rack. "Was there something you needed? We like our temps to stay close to their office, unless there was something you needed. Was there?"

"I was trying to find the mailroom," he said.

"The mailroom already? My, you're taking to this job well. This is not personal mail, is it?"

He shook his head no.

"Good. I didn't think so. The mailroom is on the third floor. This is the seventh." She smiled at him. "You'll need to go downstairs."

"I'll use the elevator."

"That would be a good idea."

The receptionist's map showed a clear path to room 7102 but a wall had sprung up where the open hall should have been and he was diverted down a long, carpeted corridor that wasn't displayed. The end was lost from sight, the wall, a dusky color, curved to the right. The surface of the wall paper had the same pattern of gold suns that he had noticed on the letterhead, on the breast pocket of the man in accounting, and on the wall of the cubicle. He walked in an arc broken by doorways that led to...? Suites, perhaps, but they had no numbers, no markings, no indication of what lay beyond, only wide strips of unblemished gold across the middle of each door and on the doorframes, themselves fashioned as monolithic gateways. Someone had spent a great deal of money on ornamentation, creating incised friezes, each one dominated by an elaborate carving of a figure he didn't recognize. Yet the same figure, forward-facing and sexless, sat atop every door, welcoming perhaps, or warning, who knew?

The ceiling was high and hidden in shadow with light fixtures set into recesses every twenty feet, each one a different primitive figurine. Many of the bulbs were not lit. He walked from pool of light into darkness, then briefly into another pool of light. At intervals, a measure of natural light came in through narrow portals cut way up toward the ceiling, where a band of abstract carvings ran along as well. The glass was opaque, etched with the sun logo, nothing from the outside visible.

Eventually, the corridor brought him around in a complete circle and he found himself back at the receptionist's desk. She sat before a golden bezant of the sun connecting calls, a headset flattening her hair, a small, flesh-colored plug in her ear, a thin tube of a microphone extending to her mouth. "Foundation, hold please. Are you back?"

"Pardon?"

"I said, are you back. I'll connect you now. Foundation."

She had excellent posture and wore a modest, white blouse with a high collar underneath her gray blazer. She, too, had the flaming sun logo emblazoned on the breast pocket.

"This map doesn't seem to be accurate," he said.

"One moment please. Foundation. How did you find it this morning?"

"I don't remember. I mean I don't remember that it was this difficult."

"You should have left bread crumbs." She laughed loudly. "Foundation," she said. "Bread crumbs. Like… Yes. There's no one here by that name. Go left then right then left again."

"Are you speaking to me?" he said.

"Foundation. One moment please." Her phone rang and she clicked buttons on the keypad disbursing the calls to the proper extension. "Of course I'm speaking to you. Who else would I be speaking to? 7102 is the first office you'll come to," she said. "Foundation. I'll connect you. Try again. Maybe you'd like to have lunch with me tomorrow? Foundation. 12:30. There you are now, sir."

But there still was no room 7102, just an alarmed fire door that went off when he pushed it open. It slammed shut but kept ringing. He put as much distance between himself and the door as he could. He kept walking taking random rights then lefts. Secretaries wearing gray blazers looked up from their desks when he walked by. He kept going, moving enough air to sweep several pieces of letterhead off a desk. "Hey," someone shouted. Then he was back at the elevators, a sign to his right pointing to reception. He set off three more times and ended back by the elevators. Finally, someone from the mailroom came by with a cart and showed him the way.

The next day he continued trying Lynette twice each hour. He had the number memorized by now and was able to punch it in without consulting her phone book. He was good with numbers—they came to him easily, stayed with him. Naming troubled him, faces eluded him—but numbers he always remembered.

Late in the morning, the phone was finally answered. "Benny, is that you Benny?" she said.

Her voice was raspy. What must the inside of her throat look like? Her lungs, black from a lifetime of smoking.

He introduced himself and she said, "I thought you were Benny."

She didn't explain who Benny was, but she told him something about the job. "I call them my pinks, those little halfsheets," she said. They were in all the cabinets, in piles under the desk, folded in the drawers, stacked beneath the plants, stray sheets of pink against the walls, under the typewriter, stuffed in the blotter on the desk. Lynette said, "I abstract the contracts on pinks. When I get a full set I do a summary."

He took notes. Contracts, pinks, summary.

Before he had a chance to ask for clarification or more information, she said, "Start with pile to the left of the desk closest to the telephone right beside the typewriter. See it?"

There was no pile to the left of the desk closest to the telephone right beside the typewriter, he had eliminated it hours ago.

"Yes," he told her.

"Go through that. Do pinks. You can call me whenever you have a question. Okay, dear?" And she hung up without saying any more, without explaining how he should deal with the massive piles, or what she did, or what he really needed to know to fill in for her.

In the middle of the afternoon, a small man of around fifty or maybe older came by pushing a creaking mailcart. "So there's someone here," he said. The mailcart crashed into the wall. "Damn that wheel," he said. "Can you believe they won't get me a new one?" He pulled the cart away from the wall, manhandled it into the center of the hallway. "That's better now. Let's see, lemme see, lemme see..."

The temp put down what he was working on. At that moment the light began buzzing. Not quite buzzing, more like a vibration felt at bone level, behind the teeth.

"I have more things for you," the mailman said. He went through stacks of mail pulling out a sheet of paper from one pile, gathering together files, envelopes of various sizes, mostly beige, Lynette's name written on the front.

It was hard to concentrate on the incoming mail, hard to concentrate on what the mailman was saying. The subtle vibration continued. Sometimes the writing was neatly printed, in other cases it was barely legible and slanted upward or downward according to the level of anger or distress or boredom of the sender. The vibration continued. Nothing in the bank of florescent lights recessed into the ceiling moved or shook or otherwise seemed out of place.

"I didn't bring anything for you this morning because, well, where would I put it?," the mailman said. "Get it? Where would I put it? That's a little company humor. I'm the company humorist. I'm Eddie. I haven't been here as long as your Lynette, but I've been here a pretty long time."

He gathered himself up to his full five foot, seven inch height, stuck out his chest, and pointed a thumb at himself.

"I run the mailroom," he said. "The whole thing myself. We service all the floors in the building, twice a day, on time, rain or shine. I think we should go for a third run, but I can't get any upper management support for that idea. But they'll come around.

"Got the promotion not long ago. I'm moving up. I've got plans. This is one step in the organization. One step accomplished, many more to go. How about yourself?

"I have my boys who deliver the mail, but I like to get out and get around. Keep my finger on the pulse of the company, if you know what I mean. We hear and see everything, first, in the mailroom. We know who's coming in and who's coming out. I like to stay in the flow. It's important to know who is and who isn't."

"Who is and who isn't what?" said the temp.

"You can bet the light," Eddie said. "Got plenty more files for you. Are you ready to have me take any away?"

The vibration had stopped, or faded so low as to become part of the natural background sounds of any office building.

Eddie said, "Well, there's a procedure for it. There's a procedure for everything here. You gotta fill out the forms. Did you find the forms?

"Why don't you ask your Lynette. She's the one who knows. Knows everything, and makes sure you know she knows. She must have been some beauty. Well, time is wasting, can't talk to you all day here. Things to do. We all love her you know. Love her to death. So you do that. Fill out the forms, do things right, and we'll get along, though I can't say how much longer you'll be seeing me in this job. I'm moving up, you know."

After Eddie left, the temp thought the vibrations were beginning again. He put his ear to the wall but heard only his blood. He might have imagined everything. Whether it had ever happened or if it happened again didn't matter—temporary employees had no right to complain about the working conditions, except something as extreme as smoke pouring out of the ventilation system—but a minor vibration, not quite a buzz, a continuing pulse...

Sally shouted from the hall, "Don't listen to him," which brought the temp to the door. "He's been here twenty years. Some people do and some people don't. We feel sorry for poor Eddie."

"What about you, Sally, are you moving up?"

She looked at him for a long moment, then burst out laughing. "Moving up, that's funny. You're really quite funny, aren't you. No. I'm not moving up. I like it where I am. Funny."

He arrived promptly the third morning a few minutes before nine and took the elevator to the seventh floor. He had on a gray suit, but this morning everyone else wore some variation of black. All of the blazers and the jackets had the sun emblem on the breast pocket. One man carried a briefcase that had the logo embossed across the entire front in carefully tooled leather.

The temp exited the elevator and entered the corridor. This morning it seemed better lit. He walked close to the wall and looked down at the curve in the floor. In this way his motion seemed exaggerated as if he walked at thirty or forty miles an hour. The floor raced along and he could imagine himself inside a vehicle looking down. He zigzagged from wall to wall. He put his arms out and changed the image, pretended he was in a plane flying down the corridor, though he refrained from making engine sounds, then he was the plane, a glider only.

One of the doorways opened and a woman came out of a suite, suddenly. She saw him with his arms in wing position. He dropped them and walked on, hunched his shoulders and hurried, two lefts and a right and he found room 7102.

The chair felt more familiar. He had raised it to accommodate himself. The plants were dying. A few more days without water would reduce them to twisted husks in brown ceramic pots, the planters' earth gone to dust. He had to remember. He opened the drawer to find a piece of scratch paper and saw Lynette's rosary beads. He took them out, wound them around his hand. Their blackness made his white skin look all the lighter. He rolled one of the beads back and forth between the pad of his thumb and index fingertip. He let them slip through his fingers. He curled his fingers in and let them slide down his palm. He touched them to his wrist, to his face, tapped them against his teeth, then he held them between his lips. He wound them, unwound them, wound them again, slipped them off his fingers, folded them into a bundle in his hand, clicked them together.

He put the beads back in the drawer and got to work, back to sorting files, typing labels, separating out each project by name.

Ms. Finestein was at the door. "Is this working out?" she asked.

The temp looked up. He was startled. No one knocked, announced themselves. "Pardon?"

"Is this working out?" she asked. "Have we made the right decision with you? Are you finding the way?"

He lifted a group of files. "Sorting," he said. "Sorting and typing."

"I had a report that someone was 'fooling around' in the hallway," she said. "Was that you?"

"I've been here since nine," he said.

"Flying. Pretending to fly. Sounds like unbecoming behavior. Do you know anything about it?"

He waved the files again. "Going through," he said "There's a lot."

After Ms. Finestein left he found himself drawn to the beads, their clicking sound a comfort. He took them out of the drawer, held them, clicked them together, moved a few back and forth on their string. For a moment he thought the vibration was starting again, but it was imagination. He clicked the beads. What was their origin?

He took down the dictionary to look it up. Flipping through the pages to *r*, he went too far, leaping to *v*. The dictionary opened to a random page, but there he came across a note in the same scrawling hand, Lynette's handwriting, next to the word *virgin*:

What is left to me now but the workings of my hand. I have the pleasure, if I can still call it that, many times a day, and at my age, still feeling the need. It refuses to die within me no matter how dry my skin becomes, how deep the lines cut into my face, how sagging my breasts. I am seething. Imagine, seething. It would disgust most anyone to know. The men would shudder and the women would turn away because women my age do not feel such things. They are not supposed to feel, but I feel it all the time. The young boys in the mailroom come by my door and I feel. I look at them. It is inevitable that my eyes leave the pages of my work, drawn to them, and I feel. One of them, Martin is his name, attracts me the most. He is a foreign boy with dark hair and dark eyes and a fringe of lashes that circle his eyes. I can imagine kissing those lashes, holding his face between my hands. He keeps his head down when he comes into my office, his eyes avoid mine as if he can sense my heat, recognize the scent that must be coming off me, the blood smell. I have not bled in years and yet the smell is still upon me, and he must know. He leaves without a word and I wake up bewildered and uneasy. After he goes I am uncertain if he were really here, if I am really here. But the mail lies unopened on the table still bearing the moist imprint of his young hands, and I am here, feeling, still feeling, seething for everything I once had and am now denied.

He slammed the dictionary shut. Perhaps Lynette was a writer of fiction, the note some research on a character she was working on. Who would leave such writing in a dictionary? Ms. Finestein said she was very old. An old woman, seething. Then he noticed the pictures on the wall: a line of women dancers wearing abbreviated costumes, each with one long and muscular leg raised exposing themselves; waves rolling into an unknown beach, billowing in a surging white foam that spent itself upon the sand; a close shot of the stamen and pistil of a brightly colored flower that displayed a delicate veining he never knew existed; a forest scene, the dense green vegetation grown so closely together it was impossible to make out one tree from the next, the branches formed arcing boles that presented curved openings, darkness beyond. There were no gold sun logos anywhere except on the letterhead and the stacked files making Lynette's office unlike any of the others he had seen. There were other framed pictures, religious ones—of Jesus, one in which the red of his blood beneath the crown of thorns and at the punctures on his wrists and legs was so crimson as to be fresh and still pumping from a jubilant heart.

After that it was difficult to get back into the routine of the work. Seething. What kind of life did a woman in her seventies lead, alone, with only her job, a set of rosary beads, her cigarettes, and stolen ashtrays to ground her.

He decided not to call her just then. There were plenty of contracts to continue typing onto the pinks. By now he had figured out that, rather than use the electric typewriter, it would be quicker to input them into the computer, use the spelling checker, and later print them out onto the halfsheets of pink paper. He sat before the amber screen creating new computer files, typing, inputting information. He typed very quickly and accurately. He prided himself on his small muscle control and his lack of mistakes. The language was repetitive—boring. The words became signs only. He didn't consider their meaning or import. One word followed another. He was the kind of typist who got past letters; he grasped the words whole and his fingers responded.

His method of typing produced a kind of split focus. He saw the information and typed it simultaneously without reading and without needing to understand, and, at the same time, a part of his mind stayed free to wander into other places. The dictionary troubled him. Perhaps she didn't believe anyone but her would ever see the entry, or perhaps there were others. He stopped typing abruptly and took the book down, opened it once more. Across from the word *size* Lynette had written:

He did what I said. Not once, not twice but three times, I chose and he carried out my wishes. I remember exactly what those three decisions were: a dance group, a children's choir, a writer whose poetry I thought had promise. I said yes and they received sufficient funds to go forward with their art. Amazing. He told me I had an eye and ear, that he approved of my taste, and I was all the more amazed. Here was a man, an important man, an older man, a handsome man, a man with wealth and power, and within the region, a good deal of fame, approving of me. When he stroked my arm during a private dinner, a warmth spread through my entire body, and when he moved me to the cushions of his sofa in his office I went along. I didn't think much about the right or wrong of it, consider motivation, look for meaning. He murmured in my ear about how beautiful I was, and how much he appreciated that beauty, how my youth was a gift; I went along. There was one moment of resistance before I lay there completely naked before him, but he spoke to me in such soothing tones about my promise, about the future, about things that I had only imaged in veiled and blurred outlines, that I went along. I experienced a sharp moment of pain the instant he entered me, and then the pleasure; after that there was no turning back. He had created something that night, a force that he would later regret. He tasted me, yes, but once I tasted the pleasure, nothing would stand in my way of obtaining it, more and more and whenever I chose, with whomever I chose. That was the lesson of the office and that sofa, the cushions beneath me: they could not have me, own me, as they thought. My body was mine to chose to do with as I wished. Af-

terward he was tender, asking if he had hurt me and was I all right. I said that we should do it again, immediately, without waiting, and when he was unable to recover as quickly as I needed, I learned something else. I saw it in his eyes. They fear us. They fear us for what they cannot have, and what they cannot own.

He put the dictionary on the shelf. He closed the cabinet. He wiped his hands on the legs of his trousers, several times. He went back to typing. He thought only about the files and the typing until he opened a drawer to look for another pen and saw the beads once more—which reminded him of the dictionary. He knew much too much about Lynette for a woman he'd spoken to only once. He didn't fear what he didn't have, didn't own. It was something he never even thought about.

Still he couldn't leave it there. What else had she written? He opened the dictionary and found an entry across from *abacus*:

The room was quite silent, possessing too much space to accommodate my need. There was no sound from the roads or the town or the hills. The day was ending, the sky a band of darkening blue; the sun prepared to disappear. I was afraid. I stood in front of him. I dropped the black silk which swept down my back to fall to the floor with the merest rustle. I parted my legs. I stood before him naked and young and wanting and he didn't raise his eyes to me, didn't raise his eyes from the floor. He continued watching one bare smooth patch of wooden floor though he could have had me again and again. But not like the first time. I wasn't willing then. He had to use a measure of persuasion and then the force of himself to finish. Now I wanted it, wanted him again and there was no holding me back. He kept his eyes down. He stayed like that for a long time. I brought my legs together and then I left him, moved to the wall, pressed myself back against it to feel something solid behind me. He asked me about the runners, the ones who swept by his house every morning before the first light. He heard them from his bed he told me, heard their sharp breaths; one of them ran and groaned. He asked me to explain because he had lived here longer than anyone and still he didn't understand. I told him they were people who ran in order to avoid their pleasure. They preferred an early morning kind of pain unlike him who took his pleasure whenever without caring or loving, without seeing who he entered. That was not true, he said. He told me it wasn't true but I, at that moment, and from then after, I had it within me to hear the truth—and what he said was a lie. I told him they came from the town and neighboring towns. He asked if there were any women. I told him, yes, young girls barely fifteen, and lunatics, too.

Eddie interrupted any further reading with a delivery of the morning mail. The temp received new files and handed back a good-size stack.

"You're returning these?" Eddie said. He tapped them in his hand. His neck seemed to pull into his body and his weight shifted from left foot to right and back.

"Got the forms right here for you," the temp said. "Just like you told me. Did I get it right?"

Eddie hesitated, his weight shifting. He said, "Lynette never sends this much back, never sends this much."

The temp pushed himself back from the desk, crossed his arms over his chest and leaned way back. Then he stretched his arms over his head. "That feels good," he said. "Getting a lot of work done."

"She never does," Eddie said. "Never does. Never does. I keep track. I know what goes in and what goes out. What does—"

"Who is and who isn't," the temp said.

"That's right. That's right. That's right."

"I am, and those are, so thanks. I should probably be getting back to it."

"But never this much. Never this much. Never this much."

"She's got to send something back," the temp said. "Besides, someone else must want those files. They've been up here for a long time, judging from the dates."

"Are you sure, are you sure, are you sure you want to send these back? Maybe you should check with Lynette. Check with Lynette. Check with Lynette."

Sally drifted over from her cubicle not far down the hall. “Is there a problem?” she said.

“I don’t think so,” the temp answered.

“He’s returning files,” Eddie said. “A lot of them. A lot of them. A lot of them.”

“Lynette is through with those files?” Sally said. “You’re sure you’ve got everything out of them you need? It’s an annoyance to have to bring back files a second time.”

“I could...” the temp said. “Maybe I...”

Sally took the files from Eddie’s hands and gave them back to the temp. “Take another look,” she said.

His phone rang at 12:20.

“Are we still having lunch?” a woman’s voice said. “This is Veronica. The receptionist. You haven’t forgotten me already?”

He had spent the rest of the time checking and rechecking the files he had tried to give to Eddie, remembering Lynette’s instructions.

“No. I haven’t. Of course not.”

“I’m going to introduce you to some other people who work here. There’s a group of us.”

The instructions were specific and simple and direct. A monkey could understand them. A monkey could execute them. The job was specific and simple and direct, what he knew of it. Why all the mystery?

Veronica said, "We're about the same age and we try to get together a couple of times a week, when we can. Support and all, but it isn't easy. This month has been especially tough. I don't think we've seen each other more than twice.

"We've got plans. Different ones, but plans. This is only a stopping off place for all of us. That's important to know about the Foundation. Maybe I shouldn't be telling you this because you're only temporary, but you look like someone who has plans also."

"I do."

"I knew you did. Can you find me back at reception? Did you leave bread crumbs this time?"

"I used a string. I tied strings all up and down the corridors."

She laughed loudly. "That's very funny," she said.

"Bright gold strings. I wanted to fit in with the decor around here."

"You're very funny. You're just what we need in our little group. Someone to liven things up. It's been getting dull."

He put the phones on forward and easily returned to the receptionist desk. The hallways continued to look less and less foreboding. He ran his fingers along the gold on one of the doorways. It was some kind of foil plating. He left fingerprints, which he hastily wiped away with a tissue produced from his pocket.

Veronica took him by the arm and led him to the elevator. "There's a little cafeteria," she said. "The food is edible. Barely."

"That's fine."

They collected trays that had the sun logo printed across the bottom and, after they went through the line, she introduced him to Milton, Ronald, David, Stephanie, Marliese, Gaila, Charles, and Eve.

"I'll never remember all of your names. I'm great with numbers. How about if I make you 002 and you 003?"

"I want to be 007," said Veronica.

"There's going to be a quiz," said Milton.

They huddled around a wooden table, the surface marked with scratches as if someone had used a pen knife. "Vinnie, '76" one of the scratchings read. They ate hurriedly, chewing and talking at the same time.

"Denise couldn't make it," said Gaila. "I think she's quitting. She asked for more money and they said no."

"What about Peter?" said Charles.

The temp ate a particularly dry turkey sandwich, washing down the mouthfuls with a diet soda.

"I should have told you about that," said Veronica. "Gone. He found something better up north. I don't know about that turkey. The tuna is a little better."

"Too much fat," said Milton.

"Damn," said David.

"You should talk," Veronica said.

"Damn is right," said Eve. "You'd better start looking too," she said to the temp. "You don't want to get caught here for longer than you need to."

"Isn't this a good place?"

All of them laughed. Milton slapped his knees and said, "He is funny. You were right, Veronica. Isn't this a good place. Like hell is a good place too. Death Valley, your own backyard without shade. Isn't this a good place. We're going to like you."

This brought a fresh round of laughter.

"I mean isn't it?" the temp said again. "I love the gold decor."

"All we need are veined mirrors," said Gaila.

"What's wrong with veined mirrors?" said David. "My mother's house is loaded with veined mirrors."

"And white rugs and clown paintings on velvet. Very nice," said Charles. "Shows real style."

"He's quick," said Milton. "At the Foundation we worship the sun."

"At the Foundation we wear gray on Monday," said Gaila.

"Black on Tuesday," said Veronica.

"But Fridays," said David, "are as casual as you please. Although no jeans."

"No jeans," they said together.

"And gold everywhere," said the temp.

Milton threw half a sandwich back onto his plate. "Yesterday's mystery meat. I gotta go."

"No," said Eve.

"Why so soon?" said Veronica.

"He's got something working," said David.

"Yes, I do," said Milton, beaming.

"This man's a comer," said David. "A comer. Watch him go."

In the elevator, returning to the seventh floor, the temp said, "And gold everywhere."

"And gold everywhere."

"Like hell on earth."

"Hell yes."

"And gold everywhere," the temp said. "They seem like a good bunch."

"They are," Veronica said. "I'll have to write their numbers down for you."

"I hope we can have lunch again," he said.

"I didn't want to tell them because I didn't want to jinx it, but I think I got a new job."

"Where? Here?"

She shook her head.

"And gold everywhere."

"I hope so."

"We hardly got to know each other," he said.

"We'll stay in touch. I promise. Don't stay here too long. You should start looking for something else. I'm telling you, this is not a place you want to get stuck in. As soon as I get settled, we'll get together. Okay. You'll see."

The office was extremely warm in the afternoon. He took off his coat and hung it in a small, closetlike cabinet. Inside were three empty hangers and a sweater that had once been white but now bore a yellowish cast. On a shelf above were more personal effects of Lynette's, but he didn't touch them except to see that there was a hairbrush, some hairspray, a pair of nail clippers, and several bottles of nail polish along with files and polish remover. He hung his suit coat next to the sweater, making sure that there was plenty of room between the two pieces of clothing.

He rolled up his sleeves, unbuttoned his top button, loosened his tie. He had to mop his brow frequently with some tissues from a box he also found on the closet shelf. He would replace the tissues before he finished his assignment, before Lynette came back to work.

He worked steadily trying to make sense of the massive collection of paper on the floor. He moved enough files to increase the height of some of the stacks to nearly six feet. In doing so, the quality of the city of paper changed, taking on a more modern cast. There were fewer terraces and many more vertical constructions. The stacks swayed precariously, but there was now enough room for Sally to get to the liquor cabinet and for him to get in and out of the office without pretending he was performing a high-wire routine.

"Sally," he said, calling to her from the door. "Sally."

He waved to her to come over, and when she did he showed her the results of his labor.

"It'll do," she said.

She had her hands in the pockets of her black blazer and was about to turn away when he asked her what kind of person Lynette was. What did she look like?

"Why do you want to know?"

Someone laughed in another part of the suite. A copying machine cranked to life with a roar of its internal workings and its fan. A door slammed.

"Is she popular? Does she have family?"

"Why do you want to know?"

"I was just curious. I'm going to be doing this job for a while and I want to do the best job I can. This could be a good company. I haven't had steady work for a while. I've been temping and all."

Sally went to her desk and adjusted several notebooks lying there. She said, "She's coming back. You can bet the light on that. She's coming back."

"Yes I know she's coming back. There's so many of her things in that office. I feel like I'm intruding."

"You just keep working. That's the best advice I can give to you."

He didn't keep on working.

He turned over one of the contracts, took out the date stamp and pressed it down five times, ten, then twenty-five times until the paper's surface was a smear of predominantly red with a mix of blue letters, nothing legible. Her tone was annoying. This might be a new kind of abstract art. His arm tired. It was enough to throw him into a situation without guidance or supervision, but to speak to him as if he were seven or eight years old... He tossed the contract into the trash. He retrieved it. You just keep on working. He tore off the last page and went to the copying machine to make a fresh sheet, which he carefully reattached before placing the document onto another pile.

He took down the dictionary and flipped the pages against the serrations of his thumb making a buzzing of his own before opening to *w*. Next to *wig* she wrote:

Nothing happened with him the first week, or the second or the third. He was decorous and gentlemanly with more than a touch of the paternal; I might have been his bright niece. He was interested in helping me, or so he seemed. I spent a good deal of the time simply in his presence. He did not have me making copies, or filing, or doing the kind of useless busywork that interns are often relegated to when those in charge have not considered why they have those young people amongst them in the first place. Several times he let me stay in his office when he was in the midst of making important decisions. He asked me what I thought of several choices, and I told him, told him because I knew no better, assumed he was genuinely interested in my opinion, discerned no motive in his question, spoke truthfully and honestly and from my heart.

He placed the dictionary back on the shelf in a measured way as if dropping it might let all of the words spill out. Then he opened a drawer and dug into the archaeology of company mailing labels and envelopes laying there. He dug through the various strata of other forms: blue and purple Federal Express waybills, orange and blue Express Mail tags, green registered mail postcards, white return-to-addressee slips, a mix of decaying rubber bands, bent paperclips and decrepit tape separating the layers. At the absolute bottom of the drawer, completely buried and forgotten, he found pictures of a woman whom he took to be Lynette. The photographs had been taken at a company Christmas party. Everyone stood in front of a small, decorated tree, holding drinks at waist level. A faulty flash turned their irises red. There was another picture of her holding a small cat, and yet another in which she rode a horse. He knew almost nothing about horses, but enough to know she was riding western, and that the animal was large and majestic beneath her.

The first two pictures were more recent, but the one with the horse was clearly taken when she was a much younger woman. Then, she had longer than shoulder length hair, a voluptuous figure, and a face that was remarkably pretty though with a set to her mouth, a sternness to her lips, the hint of disapproval. At what? Her riding companion? Nothing happened that first week. He created something that night. The man who had taken her there—wherever there was.

It was hard to make the connection between the woman on the horse and the one at the company function. Certainly, there was a resemblance, and even in her seventies Lynette was a striking woman, but she crumbled with age. Her hair had gone white, swept back in a densely sprayed curve from the roots at her forehead to her neck. She wore the white sweater, thrown over her shoulders, clasped at the throat by a gold clip and appeared to hunch inward. No more horses and rides for her. Her eyes were slits, unsmiling, unlike the others around her. She regarded the camera with the same kind of steely reserve she had used in the picture of her on the horse. She challenged the photographer, it seemed.

He would never have gone out with a woman like that. She was too bold, but possessed a kind of icy sexuality at the same time. She was comfortable in dark bars; several scotches had no effect until much later in the evening, and she smoked cigarettes all night long, letting the smoke curl up around her eyes. She understood the price of her attraction.

The woman in the picture was judgmental, harsh, and demanding. She expected men with power and money to take care of her, to treat her properly, and in return…

He found a men's room down one of the corridors. It was necessary to splash a good deal of cold water on his face. He soaked several paper towels in the stream and applied them to his neck and forehead. It helped a little. He had expected quiet, but discovered the sound of constant running water coming from the interior of the walls, as if an active cistern were in operation. It was an anxious sound, not soothing nor refreshing. It made one nervous. He needed to get out of there too.

There was a firestairs across from the men's room, and he felt he had to have a break. Except for the quick lunch he hadn't been outside all day. The stairs indicated roof access and he climbed. The door to the roof opened easily and he went outside onto a graveled rooftop mixed with clots of tar. The sun was out, and a breeze blew, making it pleasant. He had a chance to look down on the city from nine floors up. The smog was of medium thickness, banding yellow and gray off to the north.

Veronica told him to find another place as soon as he could, but why? New jobs were always confusing, and this one particularly. Two weeks work would pay the rent; he had to stay.

He went to the edge of the roof and peered over. The building was terraced as well with brightly colored umbrellas on the upper levels providing shade for a white table and set of matching chairs, the sun logo painted on the table's surface. The lower levels had planter boxes of stubby green shrubs. He hadn't thought of it when he drove in that day, but the entire appearance of the building was like a modern architectural version of a temple. There were statues out front, and the highly polished doors of the elevators had the golden sun design on them as well.

He stretched toward the sun, then bent over and touched his toes. His shoulders creaked, his neck popped, and his lower back loosened. He stretched up again toward the sun, back to his toes, and again, and again. He laughed when he realized his stretching was like part of a small ritual, bowing before a god.

Someone else was coming onto the roof just then, a guard who called, "What are you doing up here?"

"I was—"

"It isn't permitted," the guard said, coming closer. "I'll have to report this."

They were together now looking over the city.

"It's nice up here," the temp said. "Sometimes you have to get away."

"You'll need to come down right now. I said, right now. This area is restricted."

"It was so hot inside my office. I live over that way. You can't really see it from here."

"You should have placed a call to engineering. We have procedures. Now—"

"You've never been a temp before, have you?"

"A job is a job," the guard said. "If you call, they'll fix the air-conditioning, if that's what you need. You can bet the light they will. No one's probably told you that or anything else. Didn't they give you the book."

"No book. No rules. I'm making up my own as I go along."

The guard rocked forward and back, toe, heel. He looked at the door leading to the roof, back to the temp, then out over the city. "Typical," he said. "At the Foundation, there's a way of doing everything. If you stay with us, you should find that out. Now, double time, back down the stairs. I have to continue my rounds."

In the office, he opened the dictionary again, flipping the pages and there, across from the word *bitch* was another note:

One night, I asked him if he could do it with his hand, but without coming close to me, without looking, pretending I wasn't there. He said no. He never did anything like that with a woman, or by himself. It was immoral. This made me laugh because, of course by then, I could hear the truth and the lie in what he said. They are so transparent, men, holding to their rigid positions and asking, no demanding you believe. What liars, all of them. He said he felt badly about my having asked. What kind of woman was I? What kind of person? Such questions from a man who takes the only thing a sixteen year old virgin can claim for herself until she enters the world of men, took it by force, and not only the front but the back, as well, filling all of me, telling me that this is real love. He couldn't agree, he said, because if he did, he wouldn't want to see me again, after. Those were the kinds of things best left for whores. He might hurt me, he said. He might have to hurt me. I could tell him about hurt. When he sleeps with his broad back to me, I could tell him about hurt. That broad back invites me to gore it, impale him on the blade of a simple kitchen knife as he has impaled me. Instead, I do it with my own hand, letting him watch, pretending he is not there. What is the name I cry out at the end of pleasure? He wants to know. But there is nothing to tell him. I do not know myself.

He closed the dictionary much slower this time, something made him open it once more, and he flipped to another page. Beside *masturbation* she had written:

Someone cried out in their sleep last night, so my neighbor told me. It was a long, drawn out cry, a kind of wailing. I told her I heard nothing, had no idea. She said there should be some explanation, but I can offer none. She said it was the strangest cry, one from the past full of echoes. I told her no one feels that kind of desire any more. It must have been a joke. Someone young must have done it to scare the old ones in the building. The neighbor went away saying it had disturbed her sleep, saying it sounded like it came from my apartment. I told her she was mistaken. I told her I slept far too soundly to know of such of thing. I was past all that; weren't we all?

He left ten minutes early, slipped out when Sally went down the hall.

It kept him up that night, thinking of her body; the disparity between seventy and youth. Who could love a body crumbling with age? How did she stand touching herself? He was only thirty, but already some of the signs were upon him. He saw the thinning hair and invested in grooming products designed to help. His hair continued to thin, its line creeping irretrievably backward, away from his face. His knees creaked when he stood up, the kneecap sometimes sticking. He needed more sleep.

He thought of the woman on the horse, taut form. He resisted, but the image came to him: her head back, letting her hair cascade in a chestnut stream, legs splayed, holding him; there was dampness between.

At the office the next morning he looked in the dictionary again and found another note next to the word *love*:

Someone wrote that when the body is sleeping it doesn't mean it is lifeless, but when I sleep he tells me I appear to have summoned death. He says there is no movement to my body, no rise nor fall to the chest, nothing that might give away a sign of breath. My body curves, but away from him, tilting to the side, attaining a new balance in the act of sleeping—or the coming death. He says that my face smoothes and takes on an ecstatic cast. The skin surprises him, relaxing into a greater roundness, a softness he never imagined, and my lips lose the thinness he so despises. He wanted a woman with a fantasy mouth, with lips that surround, big cushioned pillows to take him in, hold him there in the warmest, most intimate embrace. Now, when they are least available, they swell, assuming an impossible voluptuousness they have never possessed when am I awake. How cruel, he tells me, that I become all he desires when I lose my connection to this world, to him. This is what hurts him so, that look of joy. He cannot drag it out of me when he puts himself inside. He subjects himself to Olympian trials: he will not come before me. He will keep his head between my legs as long as it takes—and it always takes too long. He would utilize an assortment of plastic wands—if I had not stopped him. No amount of movement back and forth, in and out can do it he says. What must I dream? he wants to know. Where am I then? I could be sleeping or I could be dead. He can't tell. I say there is no difference for me. I say there will never be a difference for me. I tell him he has me the way he wants me, without love for him, only the body.

He frittered away the morning, finally calling her before noon.

"Benny?" she asked.

"No," he said. "It isn't Benny."

"I'm waiting for Benny to call," she said.

"I'll only keep you a minute."

"That's all right, dear. This is a work call. You ask me whatever you need. You keep me on as long as you have too. I'm all yours."

He asked a couple of obvious questions about the filing and then he said, "What was the company like, before? I mean you've been here so long. Things must have changed."

"It's always been the same," she said, "though Mr. Jordan is really no longer involved. Are you making progress with pinks?"

"Who is Mr. Jordan?"

"You can't do anything without the pinks. They're the key to my job. I'm lost without them. Everything is on the pinks."

"Yes," he said. "I'm keeping up with the pinks."

"Mr. Jordan was an important man. I knew him, some. He traveled, more when he was young, saw other cultures, decided we had to support ours. He was particularly fond of South America."

"But things can't always have been the same."

"When I started, everyone seemed to be excited about their work. Mr. Jordan came to my office frequently. I learned a great deal about the way men in business work. There were no buildings around ours, only a few houses, and the neighbors were scandalized. Mr. Jordan had too much money to care. But you don't want to hear about this."

"I do."

"I need to tell you more about the job. I'm the person who keeps track. Have you realized that yet?"

"There are so many files."

"Everything comes to me, through me. Now it will go through you. No need to be afraid of it. I'll tell you how."

"Maybe I should bring some things out to your house, your mail—"

"That wouldn't be a good idea. I'm not really feeling up to visitors. You call me, though. Call me when you need me. I will tell you what to do. It'll be all right."

At the end of the second week, he had lunch with Milton, Ronald, Levy, Stephanie, Judith, Denise, Albert, and Terri. David had quit to move back in with his parents. Marliese had simply stopped showing up. Charles and Gaila ran off to Las Vegas to get married, and Eve had been in a car accident and was laid up.

"That's not right," said Milton. "It was an ATM robbery."

"I heard," Denise started, "well, I don't even like to say. One of her boyfriends beat her up."

"A girlfriend caught her in bed with a boyfriend and beat her up."

"Are you sure?" said the temp.

"Beat both of them up," said Terri.

The temp said, "Veronica told me one of Eve's older woman clients tricked her, had another person waiting. They hurt her, Veronica said."

"What do mean *clients*?" said Denise.

"When did you talk to Veronica?" said Levy. "She hasn't called any of us."

"How do you know this?" said Milton.

"Do any of you really know?" the temp said. "I also heard Eve won the lottery."

"She did," said all of them together.

"Yes," he said.

"And she didn't tell us," said Milton. "Didn't share, didn't offer. Wow."

"Are you having a good time here?" said Ronald.

"It's all right," the temp said.

"She's not coming back, you know," Judith said. "I took a look at her file, in human resources. Don't tell anyone, but she isn't. We have to stay together. Cancer. For sure. It's just a way not to have to hire you permanently and give you benefits."

"Eve?" said the temp.

"I'm not talking about Eve. It's Lynette who won't be back. You can bet your damn light on that. Jesus, I hate that expression."

"That's not true," said Milton.

"Don't do that to him," said Ronald.

"I'm just cluing him in to the truth. He should know. They're not going to take care of him any better than they take care of us. Christ, Milton, you've been here long enough to know."

"I won't be here much longer."

"Right. Neither will any of us. He should be making other plans. We all should."

A ten-minute discussion ensued in which Milton, Ronald, and Levy came down on the side of Lynette returning, the rest of them not believing it would happen.

"She is old," said the temp.

"Very," said Milton. "Gotta go. Let's do this again. Next Friday."

Friday, they all agreed.

The next Friday Milton was gone, and the Friday after that Ronald and Denise followed. Stephanie was always too busy. She had starting setting up job interviews during her lunch hour. Levy turned out to be only another temp, and Terri didn't return any of the phone calls inviting her to lunch.

The temp said, "Let's have lunch anyway, Eve. You and me and Albert, and anyone else you can round up. Let's keep the group going. Invite new people."

"I'll see what I can do," Eve said, but after one more lunch, she was gone as well, without a call, without warning. He rang her extension and heard a recording telling him he'd reached a nonworking number at the Foundation and to try the main switchboard with his call.

He began eating at his desk, bringing food in a paper bag from home. It was easier than going out, comforting. Afterward, he watered Lynette's plants, enough to keep the earth moist. They looked better after a few days, though they still listed to the right.

With his first few paychecks he had managed to supplement his wardrobe and he now wore gray on Monday, black on Tuesday, blue on Wednesday, pinstripes on Thursday, and on Fridays a brown sportscoat over khaki slacks. His coats did not have the sun logo on the breast pocket, but Sally noticed.

"You're a sharp dresser," she said. "Mr. J. said so himself. He likes the way you're trying to fit in. Maybe, when Lynette comes back, there'll be another position in the department, or in another department. Mr. J. could arrange that for you." She looked around, then said in a whisper, "He's very important." She waited, as if to see if the significance of her statement had registered with the temp. Then she added, still whispering, "Very. Important."

When he finally nodded, she said, "It's possible that you'll get to meet him one day. I think you should, and I'll try to arrange that for you. One of these days. He's so busy, though, you understand."

Three more weeks passed, then four weeks, then five, and then he had been there two months. The routine never varied. He dialed her each morning.

"Is that you, Benny?"

"No," he said. He clicked her rosary beads together. He had moved the ceramic lions out of the cabinet and onto the desk with him. Sometimes he faced them out. Sometimes he turned them toward him. Other times he placed them side by side next to the computer. When he wasn't playing with the rosary beads, he found himself stroking their smooth backs.

"How are you?" he asked.

She told him she was the same, though at times she sounded stronger, on other occasions more faint, as if her strength drifted away. She worried that the job might get out of hand.

"It isn't," he said. "You've given me good instructions."

She told him she felt useless.

"Everyone misses you terribly," he said.

She said her son Benny never called.

He said, "I'm sure he will, soon," small comfort from a temp, tiny lies too, but the best he could muster. Then, like a child reading to his sick mother, he paged through the mail, describing to her the memos and letters. She gave instructions. She still believed the piles were as she left them. "I'm coming back," she told him at the end of each call. "You can bet the light."

After the call he transferred information to the computer, sorted more files, stamped documents, stapled, marked, corrected, numbered, prioritized, clipped, notated, grouped, stacked, rated, commented on, researched, tagged, tabulated, catalogued, ranked, listed, starred, scaled, copied, flagged, highlighted, evaluated, graded, collated, appended, then returned the stacks to the file room. The piles shrank. One morning, he was surprised to see a spot of clear carpet near the door, then another, then another.

The office was hot again in the afternoon and he found himself drifting off, holding the rosary beads in his hand, clicking them together. He opened up the cabinet and took down the dictionary. He hadn't looked at it for a while. He flipped through it and, in front of the word *argument*, he came across a note that read:

My first summer was a glorious summer. My mother purchased several new outfits for me from monies she had hoarded, something muted and appropriate to wear at a place like the

Foundation. She said this was "an opportunity," one I had to take, one I should make the most of, one that might be important to my future. She mouthed the platitudes that I expected, yet beneath was a genuine concern for me, fear as well. I was advancing into the unknown, into places neither of us had ever been, into places that terrified my mother because they were a break from the settled, suburban way of life she had known. I read too much to be satisfied with wide, swept walkways, white pickets, a tended yard. A rotating weekly menu and love on Saturday night did not seem to me fulfillment. So when he chose me to come work for him, I was as ready as I might be. Yes, the unknown stretched before me, and there was great uncertainty, and I had no idea, then, of his true intentions, but in my mother's tired words, there was, indeed, an opportunity for me; I had to take it.

He pulled out the picture of Lynette on the horse. He saw her in the room, watched her ride the horse, the man she wrote about. Where had this all happened? When?

He called her up and asked her about the Anchove file. She immediately said, "Is there something wrong?"

He only wanted to move some of the files out of the room. "Would that be all right?"

"There was something in your voice, I thought something might be wrong."

"Everything is fine," he assured her. "I just wanted to know about moving the files. I didn't want to do anything without checking with you first."

"You decide," she told him. "I'll trust your judgment. Whatever you think is right," she said. "I appreciate a man who has control of a situation, and I think you're learning just fine. Tell me what else you want."

"Well, I..."

"You can tell me anything. Ask me anything. I'm here for you. Tell me what you need."

"I've been using the computer."

"That was something I never learned," she said.

"I could show. When you come back."

"I know you could."

Ms. Finestein looked up from her desk. Her blue blazer hung neatly on the coat rack next to the door—he brushed against it walking in. She smoothed her blue skirt. "What a nice surprise. I was just speaking to Lynette about you. Not ten minutes ago."

"I can't tell if she's getting better. She seems to be, but I don't know. I hope so. But you never know with old people."

"What can I do for you? I have another appointment in thirty seconds, and I'm sure you have plenty to do."

"I think I'm doing a good job for you."

"We've had no complaints. Lynette definitely appreciates the job you've been doing as well."

"That's what I need to speak to you about."

"Let me stop you here. I'm just your liaison with the company. I'm not the person to speak to. Was there anything else?"

"I need to discuss the money with you."

"That's something to consult with your agency."

Phones were ringing. An assistant shouted out, "Karen Smith on two."

"I'll do that," the temp said. "But I need to discuss it with you. I was brought in to do wordprocessing and paid a wordprocessing rate and—"

"What line?" Ms. Finestein shouted.

"Two."

"Tell her I'll call back."

Someone walked in with a stack of papers, put them into a black wire basket that sat at the corner of the desk, picked up a stack from a silver basket, and said, "These done?"

"Yes," Ms. Finestein said. "You can file them along with the others."

Another phone rang and was answered.

The temp said, "I'm clearly doing much more than wordprocessing. Have you been up to her office? Have you seen?"

"Markus on one."

"Call back."

The temp fingered his collar, pulled it away from his throat, adjusted his tie. An assistant walked into the office and placed files on the credenza behind the desk. "We couldn't find it," he said. "And your three o'clock is here. Also your 3:30 and 3:45. The four o'clock called and said he's lost. The 4:15 cancelled. We moved your 4:30 back."

"It's in there," said Ms. Finestein.

"Will you be here after five?"

"You need to look again."

"Two of us have looked twice," said the assistant. "It's not in there."

On the way out the assistant bumped the temp. "Sorry."

The temp felt something come up his throat, a fragment from his last meal. Not so big as to choke him, but enough to inspire fear. He said, "I was brought in to do wordprocessing and paid a wordprocessing rate and I'm clearly doing much more than wordprocessing and—"

"Did you find it yet," she shouted. "I know exactly what your job entails."

"Philip Lowe on three and Janice on four."

"Pardon?" said the temp.

"Call back," Ms. Finestein said. "Who is holding on two?"

"No one. They hung up."

"Albert, come here."

She folded her hands onto of the desk and squared her shoulders. She composed her face. The temp watched all of these changes take place as if she were creating a mood for her assistant's arrival. Albert, who the temp knew from his few lunches with some of the other employees, came into the office. He had on a blue suit and a tie featuring the sun logo running up and down the length of it. The gold sun was also emblazoned on his breast. He bent his palm up and waved feebly at the temp.

"We've discussed this, Albert."

"I'm sorry, Ms. Finestein."

"We can't have you losing calls. They could be important calls."

"I'm sorry, Ms. Finestein."

"I'm going to have to log this into your file. That's how it has to be."

"I'm sorry, Ms. Finestein."

"I'm sure you are." After Albert left she said, "So is everything settled then? You'll call your agency and they'll be the ones to handle things. I'm glad we had a chance to talk."

"I was brought in to do wordprocessing," he said, "and paid a wordprocessing rate and I'm clearly doing much more than wordprocessing. This is an administrative position."

"Listening is an important skill. A very important skill. All of our employees here at the Foundation know how to listen. It's the first thing we teach."

"Shouldn't an administrative position pay more?"

"Are you unhappy with us?"

"I'm looking… I want… it's important to me… I'm looking for a small increase. A kind of acknowledgement of the job I'm doing."

Ms. Finestein was silent. She took her hands from their position on the desk and brought them up in front of her mouth, clasped them as if she were praying.

He said, "If I went to a law firm, I could make a significantly higher rate. I've had offers in fact."

She tapped her index fingers against her lips three times, paused, tapped them three times again, but did not say anything.

"I don't think I'm being unfair here," he said. "In your position, you have to be aware of what kind of rates are available for what kind of services."

"I'm sorry to hear that you're not happy here with us. I had hoped for so much more."

The phone rang. Several men walked by the door. The air conditioner kicked up, the breeze enough to ruffle the temp's hair. He said, "Are you saying you can't find a way? There's no way? Is that what you mean?"

"We want all of our people to be happy. Even our temporary people," she said, drawing out the word *temporary.*

The temp was silent for a moment or two as well. A workman entered the office and said, "Sorry to disturb, checking the wall for this weekend's painting."

"Go ahead. We've decided on off-white. Is that correct?" said Ms. Finestein.

"Don't know about that. I'm just doing the prelim on the surfaces."

"I distinctly asked for off-white."

He shrugged and said, "Sorry to disturb," before backing out of the office.

"I didn't say I was unhappy," said the temp. "I'm not unhappy. This is a wonderful company. I like working here. You must be aware that I like working here."

"Will you stay and finish out the assignment?"

"I just feel that there should be more… money."

"Will you stay?" Ms. Finestein said.

"I want to be honest with you. I believe I'm an honest person."

"We value honesty here at the Foundation. We value directness. We value initiative. We value value."

He took a deep breath and said in a rush, "I can't stay. Not if another position becomes available somewhere else. That's as honest as I can be with you."

"If we can secure a promise from you that you'll stay on, and it should only be few more weeks until Lynette returns, perhaps we could find something more for you. Perhaps."

Her desk was littered with resumes; he was adept enough at reading upside-down to recognize the formats. Brentley Scow, graduate of Southern-Central Illinois State; Philip Badam, Branford University; Sweta McGoviny, Director, The Howard C. and Virginia L. Cloud Foundation; Ronald Alexander, CFO, The Quill Company. Piles and piles of resumes clipped together with red notations scrawled across the surface in writing that slanted to the right, each a determination of fate.

"I'll stay," he said.

"Excellent," she said, coming out of her chair, pressing off with one hand on the desk and extending her other, which he took in his. "I'll call your agency."

He called Lynette when he returned to the office. Her voice seemed lower and more gravelling than ever, fainter too.

"I told them I would stay on," he said. "Until your return."

"There are some other things I have to tell you. Secrets. My secrets. You'll need to know them."

"Ms. Finestein said she knew everything about the job."

This prompted a spasm of laughter combined with a coughing fit, trailing off to a hacking cough that wouldn't stop.

When Lynette came back on the phone she was gasping for breath.

"She's not even a woman, as far as I'm concerned." Lynette began laughing again. "She doesn't know anything."

Later that afternoon, Veronica, the former receptionist, called him up. "I can't believe you're still there," she said.

"Where else would I be? She hasn't come back yet and there's so much to do."

"There might be something here. Would you be interested? It's a much better place."

"I kind of gave them my word."

"This would be permanent."

"Can I think about it?"

He was confused. Lynette needed him, to keep the work going for her, until she returned. He couldn't let her down. Who would water the plants?

He was listless, unable to focus on the pages of the files. He typed in a few lines, then tossed the file aside. Ms. Finestein had manipulated him into staying. Her promise was indefinite. Nothing, actually, had been promised. He was an idiot.

He took down the dictionary and looked for another entry. Across from the word *pink* was a particularly long one what extended onto the next page and the next. She had written:

He said what attracted him was my "flowing red hair," that, I'm sure, and my youth. I did not look sixteen. I had a woman's body long before. My early development was something I always thought of as a curse, robbing me of the chance at the slow discovery of myself. I did not progress through levels, losing the baby fat one year, gaining breasts the next, my legs elongating the year following. I did not go through the awkward stages of awakening where none of the features of my face fit amongst themselves and any sense of childish grace was lost into a kind of adolescent gawkiness that smoothed out with time. No, quite simply I was a child one night, the next morning, a woman. I began the bleeding and my transformation was sudden and immediate. Men followed me. Boys stopped playing ball to stare, the bolder ones to whisper lewdly about tits and ass, to point out what was obvious to anyone to see. I did not understand such attention, nor a transformation where one goes to bed on a summer night with a stuffed animal for a companion, the next night strangers try to climb inside. I had no time to grasp the changes, to accustom myself to the added weight on my front, to new curves. All the pointing and whispering and snickering and commenting frightened me—in the beginning.

It was inevitable that I be singled out by one of the older, more experienced men, someone who knew that trying to grope me in the movies was not the sure way to success. Someone who perhaps could sense the suddenness of the changes, my bewilderment and that I needed to be handled because I did not understand the power that I had been given through the changes. I had no control over it. It sprang forth from me, turning men unreasonable, making them act like dogs on the scent, and me, unable to do more than float along and wonder why. My mother never explained. She was no beauty and had never received that kind of attention. Her courtship by my father came about simply because their families lived next door to each other. There was a longtime and continuing familiarity, more like brother and sister than lovers. They had known each other all their lives; it was natural that they should continue together—each was enough for the other. With no challenge of her own to overcome, my mother never felt compelled to explain the functions of the body, its power, and when I changed so quickly, became a woman, a true woman, with such intensity, she was at as much of a loss as I to try to find some way of moving amid this new, so unfamiliar terrain—which might lead to love, but as soon as might lead to disaster as well.

They wanted only one thing from me, the men wanted one thing, they wanted possession of my body. They thought they could take me in that way, use me, control me, and in that way own me, rob me of any self. He was different. He treated me as a mind, not a body, and so it was such a surprise later, when he turned out to be the same as the rest of them, only more subtle, ten shades more devious. Once he tasted me was when it happened. But in the beginning he came to talk to a special class of ours at the school, a group of honors students of which I was a part. Men think that women who look as I look have no capacity for thought, that their intellectual capacity diminishes as their breasts swell. Yet I led each class quite naturally. I earned the highest grades long before my body betrayed me.

He came to the class and he singled me out and he offered what he termed "an internship" at his foundation, a place created for the advancement of art and literature and thinking. The kind of place a girl like me should be, he said. Of course I accepted. I've been here ever since.

The temp was surprised to see that it was nearly six o'clock. The dictionary was open in his hands and he became aware of it, aware of his leg crossed at the knee, a stiffness in his hip from sitting too long in one position, in his neck and shoulders and back as well. The cursor blinked on his computer. The files waited for him, still piled high enough for danger.

He took his suit coat from the small closet, his hand brushing Lynette's sweater. He took out the sweater and looked at it, fingered the not-too-white wool. He put it back in the closet as far over as the limited space permitted. Her body had betrayed her and she had been here ever since. Now she was old. All the terrain was familiar, and eroding.

He shut off the light, locked the door. The corridor was darker at the close of the business day. For the first time in a long time, he took a wrong turn and ended up back in front of his office. Her office—it was still her office.

He was not sure of how it started, but he began to have lunch once a week with Sally and a group of older woman secretaries who had been at the company for a number of years.

"We're secretaries, honey," Sally said. "None of that *assistant* B.S. You can call us what we do and who we are. We don't have to be any more."

This was the first lunch he'd had with other people in quite some time. He thanked them for inviting him and Sally said, "You don't need to thank us, honey, we asked you along because we need some young blood. These biddies are all tired of each other."

"Oh, Sally, what a mouth on you," said a woman named Emma.

"She's incorrigible," said Rose.

"Terrible," said Norma. "Just terrible."

"Terrible nothing. We needed someone else now that…"

Rose became particularly interested in the lettuce in her salad, poking at it with her fork in a series of little jabs, Norma looked at the ceiling and stroked her throat, and Emma twisted her napkin in her lap, looking away.

Rose said, "The salad is good today, nearly like homemade. Much better than usual, don't you think?"

Emma was quick to say, "It is, it really is. Something about the dressing. I can't quite put my finger on it, but I'm sure it's the dressing. I believe they might have used a touch of lemon. I'm quite partial to lemon. It's one of my favorite things. Lemon is. I think that's what they've added to the salad. To the dressing. Lemon..."

"She's coming back, you know," the temp said. He looked at each one of them, and one by one they looked back, held his eye.

"The food is horrible here and you know it," said Sally, "but it's cheap. That's why we come here."

The temp said, "I think it's all right to speak about her because she's coming back. You know I talk to her every day and she's sounding better and better. She's getting her strength."

They smiled at him. Sally said, "You can bet the light."

Then Norma told everyone about a new movie she had seen, a racy French comedy in which the young, dark-haired ingénue who starred in the film spent most of her time topless. "What breasts," said Norma.

Rose talked about her granddaughter's upcoming birthday party. She has a lovely new dress for the party, the prettiest shade of blue.

"What breasts," the temp said.

Rose rapped him on the arm. "You've never met my granddaughter. You're terrible too."

"Sally taught me everything I know."

"I did," said Sally. "I did."

"You can bet the light on that," said the temp.

The women sitting around the table cackled, swaying back and forth.

"I told you he was funny," Sally said.

They were all more friendly to him, when he went from the parking garage to the office, when he went for coffee or down to lunch. He went out of his way to stop and say something to them. He remembered their birthdays. "Just like Lynette," Emma said. Still, he heard the whispers sometimes, whispers, racing up and down the halls, racing from desk to desk. She's no better, the whispers said, She's seen another doctor. No better.

Coming to work was now like coming to something he'd been doing for a long time, a place where, though he didn't fully understand the overall design of the company and its complete workings, he at least knew enough of his small part of things, had achieved competence at the assigned tasks, had expanded the system, had made more of the job than what it was when he first got there. He fit in. He wore the proper clothing. He understood "the Foundation way" of writing a memo or a letter, answering the phone, placing a call.

He believed in what he thought the Foundation did. He told that to a neighbor when they ran into each other at the mailbox of his apartment complex. He told that to someone he stood in line with at the supermarket. He told that to Veronica when they had another of their infrequent conversations after he declined her offer to help him find another job. He stayed because *great things were coming.*

"Great things *are* coming," Sally had taken to saying lately, the phrase echoed by Eddie and by Ms. Finestein. *You can bet the light* went out of fashion, subtly, without a company memo to that effect, with no overt way of learning it, somehow the looks he got when he said it told him to stop using the phrase. What those great things were he had no idea, but they were coming and anyone who stayed around long enough to be there when they came would partake of the greatness. They would all share in the coming changes, in the coming greatness.

As he entered his seventh month at the Foundation, he wasn't exactly happy or contented, but he accepted the stability of the position—and there was the familiarity in the repetition: park on level two, take the north elevator to the ground level, walk around the marble columns separating elevator banks, and go to the seventh floor. There was no need to go to reception though he sometimes did simply to wave to the receptionist as if to establish that he belonged. He walked, briskly, down the long, curving corridor, past each of the gateways, the gold-striped doors, no more flying, he nodded if he saw people in the hall, stopped to talk if he saw any of Sally's group. He entered the proper suite, took a left then a right, unlocked his door. If it was warm, he took off his suit coat and hung it next to Lynette's sweater. He loosened his tie. He turned on the computer and, while waiting for it to warm up, went down the corridor to the pantry for his second cup of coffee of the morning. Sally was usually at her desk and he said, good morning on the way down, asked her how she was on the way back. He placed the coffee at the edge of his desk, far away from the computer keyboard, away enough from the files so that no mishaps might occur. He checked Lynette's plants and, if the soil was dry, watered them. Then he called up the word-processing program. He opened up the first file, moved a contract, turned pages. He worked steadily at his desk from before 8:30.

There was no longer much need to call Lynette because she had stopped telling him anything new about the job, though he still did at least once a day because he liked her. He called her even if it was to ask the same question he'd asked the day before or the day before that—and she never seemed to notice, or if she did, she never said anything about having to tell him the same thing more than once. What he couldn't understand was how she had continued doing what she was doing for so long. She didn't seem to do much of anything except shuffle files. He never said this to her because of his attachment and because he didn't want to hurt her feelings, and because he might discover, at a deeper level, what the job was about. He was convinced there was more and she simply couldn't articulate it to him. What else would keep someone working so long, so patiently, for so many years? There was a secret, he was sure.

Then came the morning when he got an insistent phone call demanding to speak with her.

"I wasn't notified of any of this," the voice said.

"I'm sorry about that, but I've been here for more than six months now, closer to seven. It isn't a new situation."

He leaned back in his chair and took a sip of his coffee. He tapped his desk with a pencil keeping time to the words of a little song he had made up about the sun logo. The sun, the sun, it's fun. Awful, but it made him laugh.

"Are you trying to get smart with me?"

He put the pencil down and concentrated on the phone. "I'm trying to do the best job I can."

"Will Lynette's absence affect The Report? Will The Report be delayed? We can't have The Report delayed."

"What report, sir, and please, let me have your name and number. I'll call Lynette immediately."

"The Report. The Report. How can you not know about The Report? Surely they must have told you about The Report? Lynette must have told you. Didn't they tell you anything? What are you doing up there? You temps are all alike."

The temp didn't say anything for a moment. He took out Lynette's rosary beads. He clicked them together. When he was more composed he said, "Why don't you give me your name and your number and I promise to call you back. As soon as possible."

"I need that report."

He rolled the beads in his fingers and said, "Of course you do. I'm certain of it. I'm sure you must. What was your name?"

He asked Sally about the monthly report and told her about the abusive phone call. She said, "Don't worry. Not everyone likes his job here and I think it's too damn bad. What does she have you doing?"

"Pinks. I'm working on the pinks."

"Good. Keep working on that. That's what she wants you to do. That's what Mr. J. wants you to do. That's what we all want you to do. Don't hesitate to ask me something if you don't know. If I can't answer, I'll find someone who can."

He was at the door of room 7102 when Sally said, "Michael."

He stopped abruptly and wheeled around fast to look back at her.

"Michael," she said, "think pink."

"You can bet the light. I mean, great things are coming. Great things."

"That's my boy."

He felt wonderful the rest of the afternoon continuing to go through the files and separate out the duplicates, sort by project, type the information onto the computer. He was pleasant to Eddie, the mail boy.

"How are your plans coming?" Michael said.

"It won't be long now," Eddie said. "I'm not going to be doing this much longer. I'll be moving out of here soon. Have a great afternoon."

Some people do and some don't.

When Lynette called, he asked her about The Report.

"Don't worry about that," she said. "I'll take care of it when I get back."

"Are you sure? The call sounded desperate."

"You have to be able to hear the truth and the lies," she said. "Urgency is a matter of degrees." Then she started laughing, a deep, hoarse, laugh from the belly that ended in a spasm of coughs that would not stop. The phone was put down on something hard. He waited and it was more than five minutes before she came back on. "That was a bad one," she said.

"Are you all right?"

"Not your fault. I have to talk to you later. It kind of wore me out."

Later, he opened up the dictionary again and flipped through the pages. Next to the word *beauty* was another note in Lynette's hand:

Let no one tell you that growing old—in this country—is a state of grace. Young faces and lithe bodies spring out from the pages of every magazine. We are supposed to disappear into the background, sexless aunts who deliver up the birthday check each year with no one and nothing to satisfy that incessant itch. I rode horses as a girl and as a young woman. Yes, I enjoyed the feel of the powerful beast between my legs. A cliché perhaps, but aren't clichés restatements of old and continuing truths? The first man in my life, after my father, loved to see me ride. He, himself, was uneasy on the back of a horse. He never understood how I maintained my control. But the animal submits to your will. It is the same in bed. I let him control me because I wished his domination. I enjoyed, no, I relished the press of weight on my chest and stomach and loins. I loved the immobility and yet I turned my hips, snapped them back and forth, moved them as he moved within me. We ground each other down until the pleasure came from a small place in the center of me, but it came from all places across me. For me, the end was similar to the masculine release. I loved with the body, but every muscle fired, and after my release, I could do no more than lie still and let him lean on me, his breath coming hard and his pride too that he had made me give up such control. This is the measure of love, the willingness to submerge, to submit, to allow another inside. He never understood such gifts.

After that, Michael closed his door. After that he closed his door and sat still, the rosary beads in his hands, his hands in his lap. He counted his breaths.

He thought about The Report. He had done nothing, and it troubled him. He thought about it during the day, and when he was at home, deciding it must matter. All this typing, the moving in and out of files, couldn't be the sum of a life. Fifty-three years and what had she to show? Her work was intangible and therefore so was her life. She kept a picture of a woman on a horse, a set of rosary beads, a dirty sweater. He saw her as ending up empty, lacking everything, but words. The Report must be what mattered. At least it would be a summary of her efforts collected in one place for all to see.

He turned all his attention to its construction. He got a book on presentations. He said nothing of it to Sally or to Lynette or to anyone else. He undertook its creation, its design and form.

Sally stood at the door and said, "Where have all the files gone?"

He was not startled. He had trained himself against the sudden interruptions, the arrivals without knocking or announcement.

He tapped the computer. "I know quite a bit about this sort of thing. I'd be happy to explain it to you."

She held up her hand to ward him off. "What have you been doing in here?"

"I don't mind. It's one of the things I particularly like talking about. It wouldn't take long and maybe you could use it, apply it to what you do. What do you do, Sally?"

"Where are the pinks?"

He tapped the machine, again.

"Where are they?"

"They're in here," he said. "Figuratively speaking.

"You've told Lynette about all this?"

"And I have The Report."

"And she agrees?"

"Simkins sent through a memo, though it took a long time to get ready. I kind of had to make it up as I went along, but I think everyone will be happy with it. It's comprehensive."

He held up a pile of papers, carefully stapled together, waving it.

"All here," he said, "and I think it fits in perfectly with all you've been telling me about the great things that are coming. Now we'll be able to see that they're coming."

"What do you mean, all here?"

"I even came in on Saturday."

"Saturday?" She started into the room, then she went back into the hall, then back into the office. "No," she said. "I don't think so. I don't."

"And great things are coming too. And you can bet the light. And this report is part of all of that. Lynette will be a thousand times more efficient when she gets back here. She'll be able to turn out reports like this in a day or so. She'll be able to provide information she's never provided before. She'll be a foundation of information. She'll be valuable… she'll be very efficient. And that's important."

"Efficient? This isn't what you're supposed to be doing. You're trying to take her job."

Michael sat back in his chair and blinked his eyes rapidly. "Take her job? Whatever are you talking about? I've spent hours, days trying to understand, trying to do her job, to help her out. How can you say something like that to me? After all our lunches."

"We're not going to stand for this," Sally said. "We're not. She's coming back and you can't take that away from her."

He had the beads out and began clicking them together. "I'm just trying to be part of things," he said.

Lynette called only a few minutes after Sally left the office. "You can't do it," she said.

"Why are you all doing this to me? I'm trying to help you."

"Sally said some things. They're not true, are they?"

"You told me to do what I thought needed to be done," Michael said.

"I told you to leave it alone. Why couldn't you leave it alone?"

"You told me a lot of things. You told me I have to tell the difference between truth and lies. All the things you taught me."

"Wait. That's what's important."

He sent The Report anyway. It was his, what was asked of him. The next day Eddie came by the office five times. "You sent The Report," Eddie said, each time.

"Yes," Michael said. "I did."

"You sent The Report," Eddie said.

The fifth time Michael became exasperated. "Are you in charge of reports? Is this part of your plan to move up?"

Eddie retreated into the corridor, Michael followed.

"Do you have to keep asking? Do you? I'm working here, in my office. I'm trying."

Eddie ran off with his mailcart shouting, "It's not your office. It's not your office. Not. She's coming back. Not your office."

"This is not your office," Sally said, coming over from her cubicle. "Lynette told you not to."

There was the same coldness to her expression as on his first day of work at the company. In all this time nothing had really changed. From his angle in the hall, he saw his face reflected in the gold of the door. He saw himself there, but he knew it wasn't his face, not the name, but a trick of things captured by light.

"I'm not feeling well," Michael said. "I'm going to have to go home."

He went into the office and pulled his suit coat from the closet. Then he put Lynette's rosary beads into his pocket and took the dictionary down from the shelf.

He didn't come in for the next two days. He spent the time at home reading through the dictionary completely. The first entry he found was by the word *continue*:

It was the swelling that did it. It changed the way he looked at me. I could see it in the way he averted his eyes in my presence. He no longer touched me, no longer reached for me as if my body had become tainted for him, yet it was his I carried.

There was very little written at the beginning and at the end, but Lynette had concentrated heavily on the center. Almost every page had another entry. Nothing in order. He had to piece that together. Sometimes they were as brief as "Mr. Jordan took me in his office. He had me show myself while I sat on the couch, but he would not touch me, he refuses to touch me—and he never asks about the boy. He doesn't want to know about the boy, won't have anything to do with the boy, believes the boy is not his. But who else's might he be?"

She wrote at length about the slow demise of their relationship, the increasing lack of physical contact, the closeness that had been replaced with a monetary arrangement for her welfare and that of the boy's. She had named him Benjamin. It was Mr. Jordan's middle name, which made him furious. He didn't talk to her for weeks after he found out, but the money never stopped.

She took other lovers, eventually. She was explicit about this, but they never lasted. None of them gave her the grand passion of her first, of Mr. Jordan.

The boy grew up, resenting having no father, resenting the parade of men that came through his mother's house. The boy and the mother grew apart. She wrote about this. She wrote about the diminution of her physical self, but the desire never waned. She was reduced to writing in the dictionary; Benny never called.

She had her friends from work. She had her plants, her newly found belief in God. She did her job. That was her life.

She wanted it only to go on and on, without a ripple, without anything to disturb the placid surface that had taken so much pain and effort to construct over the years. The coughing was a bad sign and it worried her. She wanted to live out her days. She wanted nothing else to change. Then she became ill.

He came across one more entry by accident; it was written on the back cover, alone, without a connection to any other word in the dictionary. She wrote:

I have been here so long I have forgotten how and why. It seems that this room, this company, is the only home I have known. My old friends are gone. Even the man who kept me here as a trade—a career for my silence—is gone as well. But I endure. When I was young, I gave myself freely to him. He was the first. Not the last, oh, no, but the first. His unique position with me gave him a charm and a power that far exceeded his natural gifts. I let him do to me what he wished, anything to keep me in the field of his attention. I can speak of him now, speak of a lover's beauty. With my eyes shut, I can see the image of him in its perfection. I see his dark complexion next to mine, his black hair. Imagine my sadness when his hair turned white, his skin too. What sadness as his power faded, his hold over me departed. By then, of course, he had discarded me long before.

When he returned to the office Sally greeted him effusively. "How are you feeling, Michael?" she said. "We missed you.

The work just piles up when you're gone. Lynette's been calling and wondering about you. She's concerned also."

"Thank you," he said. "I guess I should start in."

"Yes, probably. By the way, Mr. J. said to commend you on the job you're doing. He told me that specifically."

"Thank you," Michael said.

Eddie came by with the mail. "A lot of files," he said. "Heard you were under the weather. Hope everything is okay."

"Everything is better," Michael said.

"Good. Good. That's good to hear. See you later."

All morning Michael waited to hear from Ms. Finestein, to hear from his agency. He was sure he was going to be fired. He heard nothing until lunch when Ms. Finestein called to say that he had been approved for another two dollars an hour. There was no mention of The Report. She said only, "Because of the job you've been doing, we're moving you into the advanced temporary status. No health benefits, but you get paid for national holidays. Congratulations."

The city of paper was gone, the carpet clear, the office grown in size. Eight months had passed and he managed to reduce the piles to one stack barely five inches high, which easily fit on one corner of the desk. The windowless room was still too hot in the morning, too cold in the afternoon, but it was no longer a dumping zone for unread files, unsorted paper.

The office had become—an office, a small, out of the way office with personal memorabilia hung on the walls, along with a couple of religious artifacts. The walls needed painting. This was especially apparent in the corners high up and at the floorboards. There were cracks and in some places the paint was coming off, chipping away to yellowed plaster beneath.

Eddie dropped off three files in the morning, sometimes more in the afternoon, and Michael was able to go through the information, take out what he thought he needed, send the materials back to the file room, almost immediately.

Then everything was gone, noted on the computer, returned to the file room. The last paper he found on the floor had nothing to do with business. It was a prayer for the soul. Lord, open our lips and inflame our hearts and cleanse them of useless and evil thoughts. He didn't believe in any of it. Enlighten our minds, that we may seriously meditate on Thy sufferings and death, and the pains endured by Thy most Glorious Mother. He called Lynette to tell her she could come back now because the work was done, but there was no answer. Let us commend to Him and His Holy Mother the souls in Purgatory especially all those who have no one to pray for them. He called throughout the day and still there was no answer. We believe in God, the Father Almighty. He called from home, he called the next day and the next, he called on the weekend. There was no answer. The phone rang and rang, but no one picked up. Pray for him.

Simkins requested another report. He was cordial to Michael, giving him praise, telling him how much easier he was to work with. "That's the stuff of things," Simkins said.

"Is it?" said Michael. "I'll get right on it then."

He did nothing.

He took in the files in the morning, but did nothing about the report. He continued calling Lynette, getting no answer—and he waited. Nothing happened.

In three more months a new person called asking for The Report. "Where is Simkins?" Michael asked.

"I don't know any Simkins. There was a note here to call you for The Report, so I'm calling."

"Very well," said Michael. "I'll get a man right on it. It's a large project you know."

"I didn't."

"It is. The Report always takes some time, so don't expect it right away. But we're working on it and we'll get it to you. You can bet the light."

He kept trying to get Lynette on the phone. He took out the picture of her and the horse. He played with her ceramic lions, inventing little games in which one chased the other; he made them fly. He created a sculpture with the hotel ashtrays by stacking them at angles. He clicked her beads.

He decided to tell Veronica he was staying on. She told him he was crazy. "Great things are coming," he said.

Then Eddie died. A new person replaced him, a young man who said this was a temporary thing. "I'll be moving up," the mail boy said. "Very soon."

"I'm sure you will," Michael said.

Someone came to his door, a young man in an off-the-rack suit that was three years out of fashion, a tie far too wide for the times. "I seem to be lost," he said. "The receptionist told me two rights then down the hall, but I never seem to get there."

"I wish I could help you," Michael said. "But I'm only a temp. Go back to the receptionist. Sorry."

It was extremely cold in the office. He called engineering and got a recorded message. He called them several times, but there was no other response. It was summer out and he hadn't brought any kind of jacket with him except his lightweight sports coat. He put it on, but he was still cold. He went to the closet and took out Lynette's sweater. He put it around his shoulders, clasping it at the neck with a binder clip.

The files accumulated in the corners of the office, piling up as he held onto them longer and longer. He followed Lynette's instructions, extracting the necessary information, but rather than put it on the computer, he began typing onto small pieces of pink paper, which he bundled together and set in various file drawers. He took in files each day, took out the information, let the files accumulate.

He turned the computer on each morning because he liked the sound of the fan, but soon, everything that he had ever inputted into its memory was out of date. There was no more need to use it.

One morning when he turned it on, there was a popping sound and nothing happened. Rather than call computer repair, he left the computer off. He didn't need it any more.

In the corner and along the wall, he let stacks of files accumulate. He began to build a carefully constructed collection of terraced towers that resembled a miniature version of an ancient Incan city of paper. The stacks rose, the city spread out through the room. He constructed monolithic gateways and drew pictures on sheets of paper that he placed on top. He was careful to keep a wide avenue open so that Sally could get to the liquor cabinet.

He wore Lynette's sweater. He typed. Once the city was built, he maintained a careful equilibrium of files, taking three in, sending three out, replacing them in the city, altering its look only by degrees. He answered the phone. He told anyone who called that Lynette would be back any day now. "You can bet the light," he said.

He found a picture of himself at home, a picture of himself when he was much younger. He stood against a wall with a woman, an ex-girlfriend, who at the time he said he would love forever. She said the same. He still loved her. Her conception of forever had turned out to be a much shorter period. He found a small frame for the picture, then hung it on the wall next to Lynette's picture of Jesus Christ.

Every morning he came in and turned on the lights. He got himself coffee and sat down at his desk. He called Lynette and got no answer. Then he put on her sweater and took out her beads.

He took down the dictionary and opened up at random. There was still a good deal of space on many of the pages. Across from the word *being* he wrote:

My name is Michael Lampeau and I want to tell you a story...

About the Author

IAN RANDALL WILSON's short stories and poetry have appeared in many journals including *The New Mexico Humanities Review*, *The Alaska Quarterly Review*, *The Mid-American Review*, and the *North American Review*. He is on the faculty at the UCLA Extension and lives in Los Angeles.

www.ingramcontent.com/pod-product-compliance
Lightning Source LLC
Chambersburg PA
CBHW020611310726
48979CB00008B/1442/J
9780979958847